Words to Know Before You Read

Let's Learn The
Gg
Sound

game
gate
gear
get
ghost
girls
go-carts
gold
golf
guinea pig
guppy

www.rourkeeducationalmedia.com

Edited by Luana Mitten
Illustrated by Marie Allen
Art Direction, Cover and Page Layout by Tara Raymo

Library of Congress PCN Data

Get The Prize / Precious McKenzie
ISBN 978-1-62169-256-0 (hard cover) (alk. paper)
ISBN 978-1-62169-214-0 (soft cover)
Library of Congress Control Number: 2012952752

Rourke Educational Media
Printed in the United States of America,
North Mankato, Minnesota

rourkeeducationalmedia.com

customerservice@rourkeeducationalmedia.com • PO Box 643328 Vero Beach, Florida 32964

Get The Prize

Counselor
Carlos

Counselor
Rain

Gavin

Amina

Yukio

Kimi

Written By Precious McKenzie

Illustrated By Marie Allen

"Gather your gear, campers. We are going to the amusement park!" says Counselor Rain.

"That's great news!" shouts Gavin.

CAMP ADVENTURE

5

"Get your green and gold tickets at the gate," says Counselor Carlos.

"Go, go, go!" yells Gavin.

"Stop pushing. Wait your turn," says Yukio.

TICKET OFFICE

7

"I'm going to the go-carts," says Yukio.

"I'll go with you," says Amina.

They use the green tickets.

Then they zoom the go-carts around the track.

9

"I like mini golf," says Gavin.

"Me too," agrees Counselor Carlos.

"Hole in one!" shouts Gavin.

"You are good at golf!" says
Counselor Carlos.

"Time for the fun house," yells Kimi to Amina.

The girls walk through dark mazes.

They hear strange sounds.

"BOO!" It is a ghost!

"Get out! Run!" screams Kimi.

They go fast out of the fun house.

"Let's play a game," says Amina.

"Give the man the gold tickets," says Kimi.

"Throw this ball in a glass and win a prize!" says the man.

17

"Great job! Would you girls like a guppy or a guinea pig?" asks the man.

"I will take the guppy," says Amina.

"I will take the guinea pig," says Kimi.

The girls get on the bus with their prizes. Kimi asks, "Won't our parents just love our new guppy and guinea pig?"

After Reading Word Study

Picture Glossary

Directions: Look at each picture and read the definition. Write a list of all of the words you know that start with the same sound as *gold*. Remember to look in the book for more words.

girls (GURLZ): Girls are young women.

go-cart (GO-kart): A go-cart is a small, low car used for racing.

 **gold** (GOHLD): Gold is a warm, yellow color.

 **golf** (GOLF): Golf is a sport where you try to hit a small, white ball into a hole.

 **guinea pig** (GIN-ee PIG): A guinea pig is a small, furry rodent with short ears.

 **guppy** (GUHP-ee): A guppy is a tiny, freshwater fish.

About the Author

Precious McKenzie lives with her family in Billings, Montana. She has never won a guinea pig but has won a few goldfish at the fair.

Ask The Author!
www.rem4students.com

About the Illustrator

Marie Allen has had an interest in art from a young age. Art was always her favorite subject in school. She loves to create bright, fun characters for children.